With or Without

Romy Ronen

CONTENTS

Chapter One: His Fantasy

Our bare feet were stationed on the rocks. We looked down at the waves as they glided swiftly between the still rocks. I wanted to take his hand and jump, but I did not know how. So we just stood there, staring at the ocean below. I wanted to tell him something, anything, but my mouth was as still as the rocks we were standing on. I knew in my heart that his heart was also as still and constant as the rocks. I did not like that. It did not fit right. My heart was beating uncontrollably. What was I about to do? I knew what I was going to do. But I did not care at all. I did not think at all. I jumped. I jumped right into my fear and my love and I did it by myself. Without him.

The water was cold, but the yellow sun was my blanket under the salty waters. As I pushed myself up, the air was freezing. I loved the chill and the excitement. I waited for him to do something, to say something, but the only thing I could hear was the sound of the waves floating around me. I stepped out of the water and climbed onto the rock. He was just sitting there, looking at the sun, as if I was just a mere cloud in the sky.

Nothing was said. I was stunned by his silence. I wanted to say something, yell at him, but his silence made me silent. I could not open my mouth.

I left Jean there. He did not stop me.

My friend June had a certain glow that never faded. Her features were dark, but her heart was made of summer and gold. She always ordered the same drink, wore the same scarf, with the same elegant expression on her face, and that consistently made me feel comfortable.

"Tell me Gigi, how have you been?"

"I saw you yesterday. I think you know how I have been." I lit a cigarette.

"Yes, I know. Just making sure. How was your day?"

"It was fine. I think I am going to break up with Jean."

"O-oh."

"Are you surprised?"

"Um- yes-- yes a bit-- yes, you should break up with him. He is quite a bore. You are such a catch, you know."

"You really think I should break up with him?"

"Yes Gig, h-he's a bore."

"Why are you stuttering?

"I am not stuttering."

June ordered some more drinks for us. We had a

nice time.

It was one of those nights when the moon was not full, and the stars were not bright. They were almost. The night was just almost.

I asked Jean to meet me on our rock, but he did not show up. I waited all night. At dawn, I knew it was over. The sun was my guide to leave. As I walked away, I knew I needed closure. It could not just be over without it really being over. So I walked all the way to his house because I had a feeling he would be there. When I arrived at the wooden door, I was sweaty and exhausted. My pearls were in a bunch and my eyes were dry as sand. I knocked on the wooden door but it was already open. I walked in and called his name. No one was in the house. Nothing was in the house. It was completely empty. I was lost and confused.

I called my friend Joseph. I told him to come meet me near Jean's house. I sat down waiting for him. When he arrived, the bags under his eyes were quite noticeable and his outfit was dreadful.

"What took you so long?" I asked him.

"Gigi, it is nine in the morning."

"Yes it is. The sun has risen."

"What are you doing at Jean's?"

"I have been trying to break up with him, but I seem to have trouble finding him. Do you know where he is?"

"Yes I do."

"Well then tell me."

"You know where he is too."

"What?" I looked at him in utter confusion. We looked at each other for a while. His eyes were certain and mine were confused.

I ignored him. "Do you want to come with me to meet Hazel?" I asked him.

"Gigi! No. You know things are complicated."

"Please?"

"No."

"Yes!"

"No."

"Yes!"

"Alright."

Hazel was frazzled and incredibly clever. Her hair was brown with tiny little curls and her dull brown eyes were always awake. Hazel and Joseph were inseparable no matter how hard they tried to stay away from each other.

Joseph and I met Hazel later that day at a birthday party she was hosting for her little sister. It was in a small private park with daisies and picnic baskets. Everything seemed perfect, but Hazel's vibrant eyes noticed little faults. As soon as she noticed I brought Joseph, she started to panic.

"Why would you bring Joseph?" She asked me privately.

"Because he is your boyfriend who you are distancing yourself from for absolutely no reason."

"Gigi, darling, this is a very stressful time for me. I cannot have you bringing shenanigans to my sister's party."

"Joseph is a bright man, not a shenanigan. This birthday party is splendid. Do not worry so much."

She took a deep breath. "Alright."

Little children ran in the park, skipping and blowing bubbles and laughing. It took no effort for smiles to spread and little wings to fly free. I wanted to be like that too. From a distance, I saw Jean. I was so happy he came. I did not know how he knew about the party, but I was so happy to see him. We started running around like wild things.

We noticed a little boy talking to Stacy. Stacy was so beautiful. She had little curls just like Hazel, but her hair was a bright yellow and her eyes were beautifully blue. She sparkled under the sun. Suddenly, the little boy started hitting her. We ran to her. Jean wiped her tears away, and I talked to the little boy. I knew what this was.

"Stacy looks beautiful, does she not?"

"No, she does not."

"You like her."

"No, I do not."

"You know, little one, it does not hurt to tell her she looks nice. Do it, and I promise you will make everyone's day."

Hesitantly, the little one ran to Stacy and complimented her. And then he ran back to his rowdy friends and played football.

I told Jean that we're all the same. Little ones and boys, and little girls and girls.

The day flew by and I woke up in a grey office with a wooden door. Joseph and a lady with ginger hair were there. Apparently I had fainted.

The lady with ginger hair was incredibly doltish. She had awards and certificates, but the only accomplishment she had in my mind was her hair. She was quite old, but her ginger hair was curly and long. It was naturally beautiful.

Joseph had left me alone with the lady. She asked me questions, and I think there was vomit in my mouth from her incessant curiosity.

"What is the last thing you remember?"

"I was at Stacy's birthday party and I remember telling Jean about little boys and girls."

"What did you tell him?"

"I told him that little ones and boys, and little girls and girls are all the same."

"What if I told you that that was a year ago, and it happened a little differently?"

"Pardon me?"

She started laughing. Apparently, my confusion was amusing.

"Gigi, you have been in and out for months. You have not left the house much and you have been reliving specific moments in your past over and over again. Some real, some false, some a mixture of both. We have been meeting almost every week but you have not improved. Your friends have been trying to help you, but nothing is working."

"We have met before?"

"Yes, my dear. You seem to always erase me from your memory. My name is Dr. Green."

"My mind must be lying to me. I do not remember any of this. How do I fix this, Dr. Green?"

"Try to remember something that really hurts. Something real. Something about Jean."

I tried to do what she told me, but suddenly my mind did not want to think about Jean. It was as if I was erasing Jean too. My head started to hurt.

I woke up the next morning and had not remembered Dr. Green. The last thing I had remembered was Stacy's birthday party.

Walter was June's big brother. When he was younger, he was a big rat. He was unattractive and a tattle tale. But as we all grew up, I saw him differently. He was polite, refined, and attractive. He was everything Jean was not.

We went to a bar right in the center of Monaco. We smoked so much that my lungs became sick and we had so much liquor that all I could do was laugh. We could not stop laughing.

"You should not drink so much." He told me sternly.

"Even when you are drunk you are uptight."

"I am not uptight. I care."

"Well, Mr. Perfect, you are drinking the same amount as I am."

"C'est vrai. But, you are a woman."

"Ha! A woman. I am not a woman, I am a silly little girl."

"I do not see you that way."

"Why not? The best thing a woman can be is a foolish little girl."

"C'est vrai. But, I have had the pleasure to grow up with you and watch you. You are certainly a woman."

"And you consider yourself a man?"

"Well I am working on this. It is harder to become a man. Tell me, Gigi, what do you think makes a boy a man?"

"Vulnerability."

"And what makes a girl a woman?"

"Strength."

"Most girls would say lipstick and Grace Kelly." He laughed.

"Well, like you said, I am not a girl. I am a woman. But I do love Grace Kelly very much."

"Confident. C'est bien."

When I arrived home I felt sick. Not from the beer or the cigarettes but from the way I felt about Walter. Jean and I were not officially over. We were never over. But I felt as though Jean was somewhere else in the world.

I was a foolish little girl in Monaco, stuck with arrogant friends and a giant rat. Il y a quelque chose qui cloche.

I always knew that something was wrong. I just did not know how naive I actually was. After that night with Walter, I woke up confused, again, to the lady with ginger hair. This time I remembered her name. But I did not know where I was. My mind was somewhere else, and my heart could not catch up. Oh, mon coeur.

"Gigi, you are improving. I want you to tell me about something that makes you smile. Something real, with or without Jean."

"I remember when I was very little I heard the story of *Alice in Wonderland* for the first time. I felt as though I was in that world, far away from the real, closer and closer to magic and freedom."

"Do you remember who told you that story?"

For some reason, my mind would not let me answer. My voice was empty. "I-"

"Try to say it."

"My-"

"Go on."

"My- Is that door made of wood?"

"No, not at all."

"Dr. Green, every door I see is made of wood. Why?"

"Answer my question first. Who told you that story?"

I started crying. "My big sister."

"Tell me your sister's name."

"Why?"

"Say it."

"Hazel." My tears were falling everywhere. They made such a mess.

"And your other sister? What is her name?"

"Why are you doing this? I know what you are doing. Oh mon-dieu!"

"What is your little sister's name?"

"Stacy."

"And what happened to Stacy and Hazel?"

"They left me."

I felt useless.

Walter, June, and her boyfriend knocked on my wooden door one day. The sun was bright, and Monte Carlo was awake for life and presence. I told them the only place I wanted to go to was the beach. It was my serenity, and I needed the water to fix my heart.

We spent the entire day and night on the beach in the water, on the rocks, lying under the yellow sun. June and her boyfriend wandered into their own world for the night, and Walter attempted to enter mine. I wanted him to go away, because I knew if I gave him a key to my world, I would never have the heart to leave him out of it. So we looked at the stars and the moon and I closed my eyes. The first person that appeared in my mind was Jean. It was always Jean, and I could not control it. It drove me mad.

I opened my eyes and walked to the water. It tickled my toes. Walter followed me and stood right next to me. I tried to block him out of my sight, but he would not let go. Walter was exactly like the water in the ocean, he waved back and forth, but no matter what, he moved around and was never still. I liked it, but at the same time I did not. I wanted Jean. I started laughing.

"What is so funny?" Walter asked me.

"I have completely lost myself."

"No, no. We all love you very much."

"What is holding me back?" I looked at his dull eyes, waiting in anticipation.

"Gigi-"

"Just say it!"

June and her boyfriend came back to our world. They interrupted what could have been said, what should have been said.

The water was cold and blue.

A knock on the wooden door woke me up. I got out of my bed, lazily, and walked to the door. I opened it, and right in front of me was Jean. My vision was blurred and I saw stars everywhere. I felt as though he had just punched me in the gut. I left the door open and walked away. He followed me this time.

"Wait." He said.

"What is it that you want?"

"I want to explain."

"Why you left for a month and did not say a word?"

"Has it really been a month?"

"Yes."

"Please, pardon me. I wanted something new. I also thought you needed to figure things out with Walter."

"Walter?"

"The way you look at him. You have never looked at me like that, like he knows everything."

"That is not true."

"Gigi."

"Jean!"

"Gigi."

"You know what? Just leave, leave as you did a month ago."

"I cannot leave. Your door."

"My door."

I woke up to the sound of a tea kettle whistling. Joseph's window poured out streaks of sunlight. I told him that Jean came back a couple of hours ago.

"And you are forgiving him?" He asked me.

"Yes. I have no choice."

"Yes, you do have a choice. You can let him go. Just let him go and tell me something real."

'Something real.' Suddenly, I remembered a conversation I had with Dr. Green. I remembered what she said. I remembered what had I suspected but didn't say. I knew it could not be possible. But at the same time, it could.

"What is holding me back?" I asked Joseph.

"Acceptance."

I was out of touch and very cold.

I had a nightmare that my blood fell out of my heart and spread all over the wooden door. My tears were messy and they flooded the house. I woke up to June's aggressive voice waking me up. I knew it was a mistake to let her and Walter stay with me. It just confused me further.

I had an urge to give up and stay under everything, to avoid everything, to turn off my thoughts. But I never did that. At least I thought I never did.

June took us to an amusement park. It was the most exciting, happy place on earth, and I felt the opposite of all of that. When we got to the amusement park, Walter ran like a child. He ran in circles, back and forth, like an idiot. He was embarrassing and childish. He took my hand and forced me to be childish too. I could not stop myself from laughing and smiling, even though I did not want to. I did not want to be in that situation; it felt shameful and wrong. I stopped thinking.

After the cotton candy and the cheesy prizes, we waited on line to ride the scariest roller coaster in the park. When we finally stopped waiting, I felt a little nervous. What if it was all too much? What if my heart would beat out of my chest and catch up to my mind? What if I started to remember?

The ride started, and it was slow and steady. I predicted every thrill and turn as it progressed, and I knew how to prepare myself. It was fun, and I felt completely reckless. But the last fall, I did not expect. It was terrifying, and my heart started to leap. I started remembering. I remembered. I knew what was holding me back. But I did not say a word. It was an epiphany, but I kept it shut.

Later that night June and I walked around and ate more cotton candy. Her eyes smiled mischievously.

"Gigi."

"June."

"You know now."

"How did you figure it out?"

"You changed a little after the ride. Your attitude changed."

"Better or worse, Dr. Smart?"

"Better."

When I got back to the house with the wooden door, I walked to the white bed, grabbed my suitcase, and left. It was late, but I walked all the way to Joseph's. I knocked on his door.

"I know." I told him.

"I know you know." He said back.

When I was younger, my greatest fear was swimming in the ocean. I was terrified. At a certain age, however, I faced that fear. Every time someone asked me if I wanted to swim, my heart hesitated for a moment, but my body was pulled into the ocean.

Hazel and I spent our summers tanning and swimming. Sometimes, watching and listening to the serene sounds of the warm waves was just enough. But one summer day, Hazel and I decided to go for a swim. We glided through the light blue waters and followed the warm sun. Our toes were tickled by fish and seaweed and sand, and everything seemed to be funny and understandable in the soft ocean. It was gentle. And I was naive. The waves started to push harder, and my heart jumped. Hazel recognized the aggression, so she suggested we go back. But as soon as we turned around and faced away from the sun, the water decided to punish us, to punish me.

I had always told myself to never look back.

Hazel was ahead of me. She looked at me in shock. She pointed to a wave behind me, and it seemed bigger than anything I had ever seen. I turned around and looked at it. I was not shocked or scared, I wanted it. It was almost as if it was a test or a risk, and I was willing to take it. I did not move for a while, but as it started to progress, I walked away from it. It was too late.

Suddenly everything was dark. I could feel my eyes opening, and I saw the water so clearly. My mouth was sick with salt and my breath was withering away. There was a part of me that thought I was going to drown, that that was it for me. But I stood up and coughed the salt out of my body. And then I stepped on something very hard.

I was pale and dizzy, but Hazel was laughing. It felt nice that she was laughing. It made me feel okay.

When we got to the sand I noticed that my foot was bleeding. I ran away. Time moved fast, and the night fell upon me. I ended up in a little park. It was dark and treacherous.

"Genevieve."

I knew who it was. He was the only one who called me that.

"Turn around."

I could not.

"It is really me."

I knew that, but I could not possibly.

"Everyone is worried about you. You have been gone for so long. Just come back home. It will be okay, I promise."

I kept my mouth shut.

"Turn around and trust me."

I did not move a centimeter.

"I know I have hurt you, and I have been dreadful, but I promise it will be okay. I will make sure of it. I will take care of everything."

I kept my mouth shut.

"Why are you so silent? Why are you silent all the time? Why am I the one who has to confess everything to you?"

I laughed at his hypocrisy.

"Do not laugh at me! You were the only one who never thought of me as a joke. I am not a joke!"

I did not move a centimeter.

"Why do you hear my words and not my voice?"

I turned around. It was really Jean.

"You have been gone too." I spoke.

"I know. But we can go back together."

"I do not want to go back."

"Then we will stay gone."

"I need you to go back. I will stay here."

"Why? Why do you want to stay separated?"

"We have no choice! And I want you to have it. I want you to be able to go back."

"That is what I want for you! For both of us!"

"It is not possible, Jean."

"Genevieve, please-"

I woke up. The sun was out, but it was foggy and dim. My whole body was aching and I felt my blood drip from the cut on my foot. It was real. I really was in the ocean and I really did see Jean. I just knew it. But what I did not know was that I was living in a dream, a delusional dream.

Joseph walked in and sat next to me. His presence made me feel safer, guarded. He knew how to calm me down.

"Gigi are you alright?"

"Yes, but my foot hurts."

"That is going to be fine."

"And what is not going to be fine?"

"I am worried. It has been so long since.."

"Since what?"

"Since you have been back to normal."

"I do not know what to tell you. I am trying my best to figure this out." I turned away from him. He was so hard on me.

"I am sorry. Would you like some breakfast?"

"No. I want you to show me your door."

"What?"

I faced him. "Joseph, if your door is made of wood then I am not sane."

We walked to his door. It was made of wood. I tried to escape, I tried to rid myself of this delusion, but nothing worked. I was stuck in a memory or a fantasy or a dream.

"What is holding me back?" I asked him, again.

"Jean."

Jean. One morning I woke up with blood dripping from the corner of my mouth, glass from a bottle of liquor cutting my very arm, and moments of agony I had a deep desire to forget. Jean was right next to me when I woke up. I asked him what had happened, because my memory was dim and foggy.

He would not speak clearly. He just kept repeating himself, saying that it was a night that went too far. I got up and looked at myself in the mirror. Blood on my teeth, bruises everywhere, eyes of sorrow and shame, hair frazzled and used. I was no Grace Kelly. I was ragged, old, demented. I was everything I hated.

The worst part was that my mind was missing information and I was utterly lost with someone who I would not be able to trust. And I loved him so.

I only remembered the outside. Lights were blinding, colorful, intriguing. The club was bursting with desperate teenagers. From the outside, it was fresh and exciting, but on the inside it was empty, faded, and pale. Jean was very much like that. He reminded me of a club, an elite club. Someone who was absolutely exhilarating on the outside, but disgusting on the inside.

When I came back home the next day, Hazel immediately asked what was wrong. She saw it in my eyes, and my scars and bruises. But mostly my eyes. She told me to break up with Jean. She yelled in frustration, "It is just enough!" I told her I would, but I never found it in my heart to break it off. So Hazel did it for me.

That memory is too painful to try to remember. Let alone, remember.

My 18th birthday party was magnificent and grand. June's house was elegant and rich with perfection. All of my friends and foes attended, and my closest friends stood by me. We drank our way through champagne and burned our throats through cigarettes and other hysterical substances.

By midnight, most of us were in a complete daze. We all jumped in June's pool and splashed around like little children. We were wild and careless. But by 12:30, it had all gone too far. Hazel shook and Jean's eyes were hurt. One of them held a gun and the other looked at me in shock. Blood fell like paint in the clear, blue water. One of them died that night.

"Gigi." Dr. Green, the red headed lady said, annoying the shit out of me as usual.

"Yes?"

"Do you remember your 18th birthday party?"

"No." I answered too quickly.

"I think that you do."

"I would not lie to you." I smiled at her. A smile always helps.

"Oh, I think you would." She said back.

Not the answer I expected. I stayed silent.

"If you just tell me who died that night, I will leave you alone."

Also not the answer I was expecting.

Alright, I thought to myself, I can do this. Just say the name, Gigi. Grace Kelly would be able to, right?

I knew who it was and my mouth opened in an attempt to say the name, the name of the person I loved and lost, but nothing came out.

"You are not ready." Dr. Green said.

I wanted to stand up and tell her that no one could control me in that manner, that I was stronger and more powerful than any other individual. But my eyelashes touched the top of my cheek and not one word came out of my weak mouth.

I left her office feeling useless. The trees in Monte Carlo hung over me, disappointed. The flowers that were once strong and full of life were now cowardly and frail. My heart melted.

Walter was always trying to melt my heart. Usually his efforts were wasted, completely useless. But there were moments that I could not ignore.

I was always a stupid little girl. I made stupid decisions, but I always knew what my priorities were. I made mistakes that did not affect my future, and I knew that. I was not a teenager who destroyed herself. I was a teenager who was destroyed by others.

One morning I woke up confused, not in my bed, with Walter lying down next to me. I could not remember what had happened the night before, but my mind jumped to conclusions. I tried my best to sneak out, but he woke up just in time.

His long eyelashes fluttered in satisfaction. He stretched his strong arms and the sun highlighted every muscle on his body. His hair was messy and dark. He made an effort to show me his tattoo since he knew that was my favorite part. The white sheets and his tan body made me feel guilty, and that made me want it even more. I looked at my watch as to suggest I had somewhere to go, but it took a lot of convincing for Walter. He insisted I stay just a little longer, and I kept reminding him that Jean, my boyfriend, was waiting for me. Once I realized he wouldn't let me go without a conversation, I started asking him questions.

"What happened last night?" I asked him.

"We had sex." He smiled, enjoying this mess.

"Great." I said sarcastically. I had not had sex with Jean yet. "I am leaving now."

"No you are definitely not leaving."

And for some reason I did not leave.

My thoughts were surrounded by images of his soft lips, his tight yet gentle grip, and his ability to convince me to continue, even though I knew it was so utterly wrong. The affair lasted for months and it was as if I needed it ever so desperately.

He would always sit next to me whenever he had the chance, even when Jean was around. He found ways to rub his arms or legs against mine. He always wore a mischievous look in his eyes, and a smile that said he was getting his way. I used to think it was the cutest thing in the world.

One day, when I was 17 years old and he was 19 and a half, I walked all the way to his house, because I knew June was not home. It was right outside of Monte Carlo, and the trees in that area were always shorter and more crooked. The skies were brighter and the clouds were pink instead of white.

When he opened the door he was in blue and white plaid pajamas with a toothbrush in his mouth. I giggled at his goofiness.

"Only you would be rude enough to come over without calling."

"C'est vrai." I said with a smile.

His windows were bright and the pink clouds seemed like they were in the room with us. Spots of yellow sun reflected on his white sheets; there was nothing I loved more than that. We stood next to his window, looking out into the streets of Monaco. Moments with Walter were effervescent.

He looked at me, so I looked at him too because I disliked the feeling of anyone looking at me without me looking back. We locked eyes and I could feel the strokes of yellow sun touch my fair skin and golden hair. His firm hand reached for my cheek. I gently leaned against his hand and smiled quietly like a child. He laughed and walked away. He was respectful in so many ways. And in that moment, I was so caught up in everything he was and Jean was not, I pushed him onto the bed and gave him everything. Those little moments became my everything.

A week later it was my 18th birthday party. After that, everything was different with him. Everything was less light and golden.

The sun blasted Jean's sheets like stars in the sky.

While Jean was sleeping ever so calmly, I tore out all the pages from Hazel's journal, because I did not want to read what was written.

She always said that it was important to read fairy tales. She would call them simple and free. They reminded her of balloons in the sky, flowing with the wind, yet having control over the clouds and the world. Hazel always told Stacy and I that we should grow up to be balloons in the sky: free and powerful.

I stopped thinking and came back to the present, but I noticed that Jean was no longer next to me. He must have woken up and left as I was daydreaming about Hazel's words. I decided to go back to sleep. Images captured my mind, and my subconscious knew that a dream was forming, even though I did not want it to. I just wanted everything to be real again.

I was placed in a bright, white space that was completely and utterly blinding. All I could see, which seemed distant and small, was a light wooden door. It was simple, yet provoking, and I knew it was trouble. I approached it anyway. I opened it, and beyond the door was a man surrounded by pastel-colored flowers. My heart was beating out of my chest, and I could hear Hazel's words in my mind: 'Bad men are dangerous.' I started to step through the flowers and I got closer to the mysterious man. He never turned around, and it almost seemed as if he was faceless. I decided to touch him, so that he would turn around, and as soon as I did there was a moment when time did not progress. And then, of course, time took its course and the man turned into a dark demon.

He never turned around, but his words were cruel and he stepped on all of the beautiful flowers, aggressively. I wanted to do something, I wanted power, but I had none. I thought his weakness and darkness would make me stronger, more motivated, but all it did was bring me to my knees.

I remembered something I used to tell Stacy:

'Kindness is power.'

I woke up looking for Jean and his quiet, constant heartbeat. But he was not there, and neither was his heart.

Hazel broke up with Joseph, for good, and instead started dating Walter. June was always with her boyfriend, Jean was somewhere else, and I was lonely. I was always in a dark room with cold air keeping me company, keeping me sane.

I decided to be reckless. I gave myself to the men of Monaco; I was dressed in all black, and my lips were painted red. My red wine glimmered under the saturated lighting of different bars, and my mind became hazy whilst my lips touched lips of different men: foreign, shameful, terrifying. I had no idea what in the world I was doing, and why I was doing it. I would lie in bed, in that cold, dark room, gazing at the wooden door. All I could think of was how happy Walter was with my sister. All I wanted was for Jean to save me.

I knew that distracting myself in that futile manner was wrong, so I left that room and went to Walter's. I had more courage than ever. When I got to his door, I took a deep breath and braced myself. My heart was beating uncontrollably, and I knew that that moment was utterly real. It felt incredible.

I knocked on the door. Walter was in his blue and white plaid pajamas, and I could feel my heart melting. I wanted to smile brightly, but I could not, not when I said what I said.

He was shocked when he heard the words.

He did not reply, he could not even open his mouth.

He just kissed me under the moon.

I knew that my heart was melting, and I could hear Jean's voice telling it to stop. But I knew that living with Jean was living under a false reality. And there was nothing I hated more than fantasy.

"You have made great progress." Dr. Green smiled proudly at me.

I did not like it. She was not doing anything wrong, but I felt as though she was surprised that I could improve, as if I am not capable.

"Thank you. I now know where I am, when, and what has happened to me."

"Do you mind if I test you?"

"No, I do not mind." I did mind.

"What is the date?"

"January 21, 1962."

"How old are you?"

"19."

"Where are we?"

"Monte Carlo, Monaco. Your office."

"What happened to your parents?"

"They died when I was young."

"Who died on your 18th birthday?"

"I-"

"Do you know?"

"Yes, but I cannot say it out loud. I will write it down." I wrote the name down. She nodded.

The night before Jean died, he finally found the courage to kiss me. It was very dark and the rain was falling madly. There was so much rain and mist that our eyes could barely see the stars or the sky itself. He called me that night and told me he needed to see me.

Before that night, we had never seen each other outside of the confines of our school, but occasionally we would talk. Usually, our conversations consisted of arguments, because we were both caught up in passion that we could not express. From the moment I met Jean, time would stop and then start again: abruptly, uncontrollably, fatefully.

I walked all the way to where he was, and I saw his bright blue eyes from a distance. As soon as he saw me, he walked towards me and without a moment of hesitation, he kissed me. It felt like a simple second, but it lasted for a long time.

I took a step back, and looked at him. I had no idea what to say. He looked at me too, but he could not say a word. It was not tense or misplaced, it was a moment of understanding.

"Was this why you needed me?" I finally said.

"Yes. But I also came to tell you that we cannot be together."

"Why?"

"We are not compatible."

"But I love you." I could not believe my words. What was I thinking?

He paused for many moments. His heart was breaking. "I love you too, but--"

"Come to my birthday party tomorrow."

"Alright."

We walked away from each other. He went south, I went north. I looked back, and so did he.

My 18th birthday party. I kept checking the wooden door to see if Jean would be there. For a long time he was not. But by 11:33, he had arrived. He asked if we could talk in private.

We walked into June's room. Little crystals on her chandelier swiftly swung. As I walked into her room with a glass of champagne in my left hand, I ran my right hand through her crystal jewels. I felt his presence behind me. He touched my back and I slowly turned around.

"Happy birthday." He handed me a box. I opened it.

It was a long chain, and a ring was placed as its pendant. The ring was golden with a small diamond in the center. It was bright and simple, just like his eyes and the ocean.

"Thank you." I said simply, with an undertone of complete shock and gratefulness.

In front of us was a mirror, so he took the delicate necklace and helped me put it on. In the mirror, I seemingly looked at the necklace, but in reality I was looking at his hands. I turned around and he kissed me. And then more.

"I will love you forever." Jean said. He played a record.

By midnight, we came back outside. Most of us were in a complete daze. We all jumped in June's pool and splashed around like little children. We were wild and careless.

But by 12:30 it had all gone too far. Hazel shook and Jean's eyes were hurt. Hazel held a gun and Jean looked at me in shock. Blood fell like paint in the clear, blue water. Jean died that night.

I will never forgive Hazel for killing Jean. I never understood why she would do something so cruel. I never understood how she could betray me in such a manner. The worst part was that she took Stacy away from me.

The days after my last meeting with Dr. Green were bearable. The clouds were less of a vision and more of an epiphany. The trees were not as bright, but they were constant and alive. I felt reborn, as if I were finally living and breathing again.

During the day, I spent my time in the nature under the sunlight. The parks and oceans of Monaco were my source of life and breath. But when the sun set and the moon rose, I became another version of myself; I spent my nights under the bright moonlight with champagne and cigarettes.

As I spent more time with my friends, I realized that everything was different. I felt as though I had moved away for years and had just come back to them. Their lives were foreign to me, and I felt incredibly selfish for not considering them when I was in the state that I was.

Joseph was living a new life. He had broken up with his girlfriend who had been controlling him like a petite pute. He was in his second year of college, fulfilling his destiny. He finally knew his direction and was utterly independent in his choices and his life. I always knew he would rise above, I just did not know he would do it when I was practically gone. I was grateful for it anyway.

June found new friends. When she broke up with her boyfriend, she received the gift of faithful and loving friends. I was happy for her, but she barely had time to see me after I was better. I could tell she was tired of me; I was a lost cause to her.

Walter was with someone new. After Hazel ran away, he went crazy, and recklessly made love to many french whores. Not prostitutes, but even worse: socialites and trophy wives who could not care less. When I found out, I was invigorated, and I knew nothing would ever be the same.

I wanted to look for Stacy more than anything. I knew she was still with Hazel, and I knew that that was not safe. Even if Stacy always loved Hazel a little more than she loved me, I knew what was best for her. I just had no idea where to go or how to start looking. I had no one to help me.

Once again, I was in need of my friends. My friends who were so much happier without me.

Chapter Two: The Middle

I stopped talking to my friends. I wanted them to think that we all just drifted apart so they would not argue with the truth, the inevitable. It took them a while to understand, but two weeks later they all knocked on my wooden door, found it to be open, and walked into an empty house. They found a note inside, which said that I was sorry and I did not want them to look for me. I hoped that I was actually being selfless and not hurting them in any way.

I knew where Hazel was. When we were younger, she would speak of New York City, Manhattan, and told me that one day she would run away and catch her soul there.

When I took my first steps onto the New York City streets, I fell in love. I felt brand new. Passion roared in every corner. Sound was loud and aggressive, but in the best way. It was bold and it was vigorous. I felt more alive and real than ever before.

I had no idea where to go. I was naive enough to think that I could walk around the city and ask New Yorkers if they had seen my sister.

I had a photo of her in my pocket. In the photo she was wearing a cotton dress with little flowers. Her smile was effervescent and beautifully genuine. I remembered how much I loved her that day. It was more than anyone could ever love another human being. We splashed around in the sun. I hugged her little knees for hours and hours, and she tickled me until I could no longer breath. I smiled at the sour irony that was my life.

I stayed in a suite at the Waldorf Astoria. I had money from my parents' will. The room was incredibly beautiful, and the door was not made of wood. The view was unlike anything I had ever seen. The yellow color of the sun and the gray undertones of the buildings gave the city a light I had never realized existed. I felt completely new and inspired.

I decided that in this city, anything was possible. When I was younger, Hazel would tell me about it.

"My sweet little Gigi," she would say, "one does not understand passion until the power of New York City is fully experienced and absorbed."

I would look at her in admiration and giggle, because at the age of eight, I had no idea what she was saying to me. But then I knew.

I stepped outside and starting walking in and out of stores. Like a monstruo, I asked every store owner if they had seen Hazel, showing them that picture of her. Most responded in fear of me or in awe of me, but one day I walked into a bookstore.

The bookstore was narrow and long, with old and dilapidated books stacked in lackadaisically. The scent was nostalgic, and the man who owned the bookshop was almost as old as the books. His hair was white as snow, and his eyes were cold as ice.

"Bonjour, monsieur. I am looking for her." I took the picture out. "Have you seen her?"

The man looked at me with his cold, blue eyes. He glanced at the photo. He looked at me again. "Where in France are you from, child?"

"Monte Carlo, Monsieur. Close to the beach."

"Interesting. Do you like reading?"

"Quelquefois."

He pulled out four books and handed them to me. "Ici. Read all of these, and then I will tell you if I have seen the girl in the photograph."

I smiled, even though it was a strange request. I nodded and left the shop.

I tried my best to understand the books, but I was not very good at reading English. Hazel taught me how to read and write in English, but I did not really understand the words. Every word in English had a hidden meaning, instead of its just being clear from the start. I did not want to use all of my energy to dig and to dig when the truth was actually right in front of me.

I walked to the bookstore. It took me a long time to find it, especially since no one on the street would point me to where it was. People in Monte Carlo were very helpful, but people in Manhattan were real. They had no problem presenting their souls to the world.

I did.

When I walked in, the old man smiled quietly. His mouth was closed, but his eyes were wide open. There was a familiarity to his eyes. I could not understand it.

"Did you read the books?" He asked me.

"Yes."

"Do you have a job?"

"No."

"Now you do."

"I do not understand."

"You will work for me."

"Oh." That was odd. "What must I do?"

"Sort books. Help customers. If you want to stay in New York City, you must work. This is not Monte Carlo. This is reality."

"What about the girl in the photo? Will you tell me if you have seen her?"

"You mean your sister, Hazel? I will let you know in due time."

"How-"

"Do not worry so much. I will tell you everything soon. Start working."

I loved working in the bookshop. It was seemingly simple, but it felt like a new and complicated world. Every day was an adventure. Reading and organizing books made me feel important. Halevy, the old man, would read to me after my work day. I felt like a little girl, and I remembered when Hazel used to read to me and Stacy, as we calmly fell asleep with our dreams.

It was my fifth day working in the bookshop. As I was sorting the books, I found *Lolita*. I remembered one day in school Jean asked me a question:

"What is your favorite English book?" Jean asked me in class.

"*Lolita.*"

"Tragic. Why is that your favorite?"

"It is beautifully tragic. What is your favorite English book?"

"I have not read one yet."

"You have not read any English books? How do you do well in English class?"

"I do not do well."

"I am sure you have read one."

"Not one." He laughed and started to walk away.

"Wait." I said before he could walk away. "If you have not read one, how did you know *Lolita* was tragic?

He smiled. "I have my ways."

I felt my heart flutter.

"Gigi." Halevy called me.

"Yes?"

"How long has it been?"

"Sorry?"

"How long has it been since your sister disappeared?"

"Three months."

"Hazel came to my bookshop two months ago. She asked me for help."

"Why would she come to you?"

"Because I am her grandfather. And yours."

"Excuse me?"

"My son is Jacque. I am your father's father."

"Mon-dieu." I could not breath.

"Please, child, understand. Jacque and I were not on good terms. But when Hazel came to me, with Stacy, saying that she had killed someone, I did not know what to do."

"Where is she?"

"I cannot say."

"She killed the love of my life! She killed a human being! How can you let a murderer take Stacy away from me?"

"I do not know what to do with this."

"Where is she? Tell me now!"

"Downstairs."

Downstairs. She was below me this whole time. And so was Stacy. I ran downstairs without a moment of hesitation. The stairs were a spiral, and each step was made of wood. My heart did not beat once; I was walking down to hell.

"I know you are down here, Hazel. Come out now."

Silence.

"Hazel!"

Nothing.

"Stacy, please."

In the darkness, I saw my little sister running towards me, her blond curls frazzled and her kind eyes wet. I ran to her and hugged her. It felt as if my soul was finally in one piece. I loved her more than anyone.

I held her hand tightly; I knew what was coming.

"Sweet little sister." I heard Hazel's whiny voice echo.

"I missed you." Why in the world would I say that?

"I missed you too, my sweet, little Gigi." She responded.

I wanted to cry and scream all at once. Why was I so weak?

"We can finally be a family again." She said.

And then I remembered: Jean was supposed to be my family, our family. But she killed him. Hazel was a meurtrier. My own sister was a murderer, my own flesh and blood. I started crying because I knew what would happen next. I knew what he had done for me, for us, and I was thankful for it, but it hurt.

The police came running down the stairs. They arrested Hazel for the murder of three innocents: Jean, our mother, Lila, and our father, Jacque.

I hugged Stacy, the love of my life.

My parents met at a wedding in 1939.

Lila was a good girl from the moment she was born. Her mother, Ella, and father, Rafi, were intellectuals, and they were very warm. She was an only child, and even though quarrels with her parents would occasionally arise, she received a lot of love and attention. She cared about education and change more than anything, and she had many friends. She never felt alone in her lifetime, and was perceived as someone who was almost perfect. She had many doubts about herself, but she would always find ways to independently reassure herself and find dignity within her soul. Her good nature and straight golden hair shone under the ballroom lighting. It caught Jacque's attention.

Jacque was a refined young gentleman, but very shy. His hair was curly, but so was his heart. He lived with his father, Halevy, and his mother, Monique, and his sister, who died when he was young. He barely spoke at all. He loved to play piano, but he kept his talents a secret. He had many friends, and was perceived as very popular, but in reality, he was mysterious and tragic. His life felt like a series of mistakes and downfalls, and every day felt like a new nightmare. No one noticed his pain, and he was happy about that, because he did not want it to change, because he knew it would only be worse. But on that wedding day he felt his heart open for the first time.

"May I have this dance?" Jacque said, five words that ultimately changed both of their lives forever.

"Yes." Lila responded, and both of them blushed like children.

They danced for a long time, and they did not speak much. They understood that they were not very compatible. But because they were not compatible, and because they had absolutely nothing in common, it pulled them in closer and made them work harder to find common ground.

It was obvious that their souls were bound to meet.

"What do you want from this life?" Jacque asked Lila with a bright, eager gaze.

"Fireworks." She responded.

He did not understand what she meant that night, but the moment before he died, he finally understood. He was glad he was able to give it to her.

Monique died in 1940. The soldiers came into their small house in France. All of their six sided stars were hidden safely in their drawer. The soldiers stormed in and opened the drawer. Monique lied for the first time in her life by telling the soldiers she was the only Jewish person in the house. She showed them the six sided stars, and since they were all necklaces, the soldiers believed her. They took her away, and her body ached from her hard, long death. Halevy's soul died forevermore.

Lila's mother, Ella, died in 1940; she hurt with all of her heart and was devastated by the radical evils of the world. Rafi, Monique, and Ella were all together in the same camp. Rafi survived, and remembered the events that had transpired in the camps. Rafi spent long nights with Halevy telling him about Monique's last moments in this world. The world was ruthless in their eyes, and nothing would ever change that.

Hazel was born in 1942. She was an accident. Lila and Jacque were unmarried and not ready for her. Rafi and

Halevy were angry that this child was born so early and in such an unsettling time. They were not ready to welcome such a beautiful child in this troubling time. When she was born, Halevy looked into her eyes and knew something was very wrong. She did not have kind eyes. They were not part of the family he loved so dearly. But he did not say a word; he knew appearances were deceiving and he would never blame an innocent newborn for the wrongdoings of the world. He kept his mouth shut, but he should not have done that.

Lila and Jacque married months later.

I was born in 1943. I was adored, even though I was technically an accident and the world was still very wrong. Halevy loved me from the moment I was brought into the world. The moment he looked into my eyes he knew I was an honest, Jewish soul. However, he decided to move to Israel a day after I was born, with Rafi. They knew that they were safer there, and he wanted me, my parents, and my sisters to move, but my parents refused. They could not leave their home, even though it was not safe. Halevy and Rafi became enraged by their ignorance. They left, and never came back. Halevy moved to New York, alone, much later in his life.

Stacy was born in 1954. She was loved unconditionally. From the moment she was born, the world knew she had the most innocent, beautiful soul. Her curls and her lively spirit brought joy to everyone.

Jacque and Lila died in 1955. Hazel was only 13 years old; she grabbed a gun from our father's drawer. She fired warning shots, but many, and it was too late for my parents. I was horrified, but she knew I would not accuse my own sister of murder. I stayed loyal to Hazel until 1961.

Jean died in 1961. I realized my sister was a murderer who deserved to be in jail.

I realized that blood was not a factor that defined family: love was.

"What do you want from this life?" Jacque asked Lila with a bright, eager gaze.

"Fireworks." She responded.

He did not understand what she meant that night, but the moment before he died, he finally understood.

The moment before my father died, he was lying down on the floor with gunshots in his heart. I ran to him, my little heart pattering, my wide eyes swelling with tears. He looked into my eyes and I looked into his. I tried my best to cover his wounds with my jacket, but we both knew it was his end. He touched my little hand and he felt fireworks. Red firework filled with love and blue fireworks filled with forgiveness.

As soon as his eyes shut, and his heart stopped beating, I ran to my mother. Her delicate skin was drowning in blood. Hazel shot her in more places, and it was harder for me to look. I wanted to put my hand on hers in her last moment too, but it was too hard for me.

Hazel stood in the corner, repeating over and over again: "It was an accident." She was not shaken or even moved by our parent's blood on the floor. She was laughing.

Stacy was only one year old, but she was in shock. Her heart was bigger than both of our souls combined.

Chapter Three: My Reality

When we came back to Monte Carlo from New York, I realized that everything was different. Everything that I had felt after Jean's death was no longer relevant. All of the things that I thought had happened, actually did not. It was like moving into a new, foreign home, except it was already home. I felt sick. How could I have imagined so much and believed it? What was wrong with me?

Nevertheless, I had everything I needed. I had my house, my little sister, and no wooden doors. I had my sanity. I had my friends, even though I did not want them.

I knew what everyone wanted from me. June wanted my advice. Walter wanted my body. Joseph wanted my friendship. Stacy wanted my love. But I had nothing left to give. I felt used and broken.

I decided to apply to university. It would take up my time, distract me from life. It was what I was meant to do before Jean died. The application process was terribly difficult, and I would not have gotten in if my grandfather, Halevy, had not had the connection he had. I was grateful for my grandfather.

I was very excited on my first day. The environment felt new. The air felt new. Everything was new.

Before I even walked into class, I bumped into a blonde gentleman, who was so blonde it was hard to use another adjective to describe him. His hair was blonde, his eyes were blue, his skin was fair, his hands were soft.

"Sorry." I said.

"It is alright. Are you a freshman?"

"Yes. Are you?"

"Yes. What class do you have now?"

"Judaic studies."

"Me too. Can I walk you?"

"Yes, of course."

"What is your name?"

"Gigi. And yours?"

"Levi."

We were friends, close friends. He felt like family to me, at first.

Joseph always felt like family to me. No matter how many people would claim we were more than friends, our bond was never like that. I loved that about our friendship.

But with Levi, it was not the same. It was different.

Jean always roared a certain passion in my heart. I would shake and shiver in his presence. That feeling was one only Jean could control; he had the lever to my heart and soul. No other person would ever make me feel that way.

But there was something about Levi that reminded me of it.

June would always give me advice and expect the best of me. Whenever I made a mistake, she accepted it, but made it clear that it was a big mistake. I needed that guidance.

Levi acted in that way. He asked me why I smoked. He asked me why I drank so much. He asked me why. And when I said I did not know why, he nodded. I did not feel inferior to him, because when he nodded it was more in understanding and less in judgment.

Walter was always very judgmental; he had to prove a point no matter what. But he was sexy.

Even though Levi was not as sexy, he was just as attractive. Levi watched over me just as Walter did, but he was not judgmental or stubborn about the mistakes I made in the past.

Oddly enough, I knew that Halevy would love Levi, as if he was his. I knew that if Halevy were ever gifted with a grandson, he would want Levi. And I knew that Levi would look up to Halevy as if he were the greatest person in the world. But that came later.

I always had to make the effort. The friendship felt very one sided. I felt that if I ever stopped talking to Levi, he would not start a conversation. That was part of the reason why I never confessed my feelings for him, because I knew that if he was not fully engaged in the friendship, how could he ever have feelings for me?

I always felt that I was not good enough, not worth it. I felt that I needed to be more of something so that my loved ones would care more. When I made mistakes, I felt even worse about myself.

I said I did not care about my image, but at the end of the day, I did, very much so.

I started drinking so that Hazel would see me as "mature."

I started smoking and using drugs for Jean's attention.

Levi made me realize that pills and potions were a joke. But I should have realized it myself. I should have been independent enough to understand that I changed myself for others.

I changed myself so much that when I looked in the mirror, I saw someone else. I decided to spend all of my time studying, playing with Stacy, calling Halevy, and spending some time with Levi when he was not busy.

I tried to spend time with Joseph or June, but I stopped seeing Walter. I felt it was odd to remain friends with someone who I had made love to. He kept trying to see me, but I refused. It was a nice change, for once.

I slowly began to recognize myself. My hair turned lighter. My eyes became greener. My face became fuller. I felt alive and real. I felt as though I was reborn: from my first life, death, and then onto my second life.

Neutral, simple, and less wild.

Wild. Jean was a lion and I was his lioness. He was wild and untamed. I was only one of his many interests, but I was known as his one in a million. Everything was wild and carefree, and he set my heart on fire in the best ways and in the worst ways.

Less wild. Levi was my garden, and I was his flower. Maybe not his, but I was a flower. And maybe he was not my garden, but he was there. I blossomed and matured as his sun and his grass and his entire atmosphere made me feel good to grow in. He did not start a fire, but the warmth from his sun was my blanket in the harsh winters. Even though it was seemingly safe, I felt at risk every second when I was with him, I felt pressure to be better, I felt challenged.

It exhausted me and it invigorated me.

Drops poured madly as the skies of Monaco rumbled and darkened. Levi and I were leaving class, and for some odd reason the sun was still shining amongst the darkened skies. We walked under his goofy, yellow umbrella and remained completely dry.

"Your umbrella is ugly." I said.

"So are you." He replied jokingly.

I could not help but think of Jean. His umbrella would have been black. His eyebrows would have furrowed. He would have sucked the air out of my lungs. It would have felt as though we were not going anywhere, as if we were trying to move but nothing was progressing. Thunder would have struck.

With Levi, everything was moving. I was breathing. The air was clear, the sun was shining. I felt new.

But that night I had a dream; it was vivid and clear. There were two wooden doors: one was yellow and bright and the other was dark.

In the dream I knew I had to choose one. I initially walked towards the door that was brighter, the yellow one. It was warm, and I could hear a sound coming through it. The sound was kind and soft, echos of the waves in the ocean.

I walked to the other door, the dark one, and my heart pattered like a madman. It was uglier, but I was extremely drawn to it. I could feel my soul expanding like hot metal.

I knew the right choice, but I still could not decide which to open. Because I knew that when I opened one, the other would be gone forever.

There was a bubble of darkness drawing me back into the depths of delusion.

When I touched the handle on the dark wooden door, it was freezing and my hands shook, but I did not let go. I turned it painfully, as shards of ice pricked my fingers and made me bleed. My blood soaked the handle's snowy exterior.

As I walked in, darkness surrounded me, but I could see everything, because there was one lit candle in the center. It was freezing; my very breath turned to ice. I felt salty drops falling from the air, and realized later that they were tears. There were shattered pieces of glass everywhere, and my foot gently bled. There were unopened letters on the floor, and when I tried to pick them up and read them, the wounds on my hand reopened and bled. Hundreds of bats flew from corner to corner, and I felt myself wanting to flee. My heart was racing. I looked out into the distance, and as I continued wandering, I saw a big, beaming, orange light. I ran to it instinctively, bloody, cold, and wet, because I saw his blue eyes waiting there for me. Finally, everything would be okay and he would tell me and I would hear the echo, his voice. But as soon as I reached to the light and to his eyes, I was pulled out.

The handle to the yellow door was warm and welcoming, and when I opened the door, I smiled, because I knew it was summer. The grass was dewy and the sun was shining and the weather made me want to spin. Levi was sitting there with a picnic basket.

Suddenly, I felt water splash my clothing. I splashed back. It was goofy and exciting, and it was the summer I never had. It was the summer I had always wanted. But as soon as I touched his hand, I was pulled out.

And that was when I knew my choice.

There was a bubble of darkness drawing me back into the depths of delusion. But I was finally seeing everything for what it truly was, I was back in my own reality. I was not going to let anything trap me.

I knew that I wanted Jean the most, but he was not a choice. I knew I wanted Levi in some ways, but I was too frightened to choose him. So, I chose neither. I took out the keys and locked myself out of both doors.

I had a preconceived notion that university would be easy, but I had forgotten what school was like. I was exhausted all the time, especially without espressos or cigarettes, and the only substance that fueled me was the champagne I consumed under the moon.

I did well in my classes, and I was proud of myself. But every time Levi did better, I felt silly for even trying. Unlike Levi, Jean was somewhat stupid; I was the smarter one. But in this case scenario, Levi was smarter. Maybe not emotionally, but when it came to our classes, he was brilliant. I felt less intelligent, and it was a feeling I was not used to. It made me feel weak and vulnerable.

One night I sat under the moon and the stars with my champagne, and Levi saw me. He was drinking too, but when he saw how much I had consumed, he became enraged. He took me home, even though I refused, and I passed out.

The next morning he was gone.

"Why did you leave?" I asked Levi in class the next day.

"I went home and slept."

"You could have just stayed over."

"You had passed out so I did not have your permission. And I would rather sleep in my own bed, thank you."

"Alright."

He was so cold that I got goose bumps.

"I have been trying to quit smoking." I told him, searching for an ounce of warmth in his cold eyes.

"Good."

Good? Not wonderful? Nothing else? Not even a dimple-filled smile?

I realized I did not need his approval. But I wanted it.

I woke up as the morning sun shone too brightly. The stench of the night before stuck to my sheets. It was stale and awful. My brain attempted to remember anything: hours, minutes, moments, but nothing.

Stacy thought I had died, since I was completely out, so her response to my 'death' was to jump on my bed. She was very insightful.

That morning, I started to think about moments when Jean and I used to laugh. We barely laughed together, but even the rare memories filled me with sour joy. I knew that thinking about Jean was my downfall. But I could not stop. It was an obsession.

The phone rang just as I had indulged myself in a delusional mindset. I was grateful for the incessant sound of the phone ringing. It was my savior.

"Hello?"

"Gigi, it is Halevy. I am coming to visit you."

"Really? Good. You can stay with us. When are you coming?"

"Tomorrow."

"Tomorrow? That is very short notice. Is everything alright?"

"Yes, everything is splendid. I will see you tomorrow night."

I hung up.

My house was as repulsive as a pigsty. I could not let my grandfather see my cigarettes and my empty champagne bottles and mistakes from nights of highs and lows.

I drank so much espresso that I was convinced I was going to explode. Stacy and I spent the whole day and the whole night removing any remnants of my inappropriate ventures so my grandfather would be proud. I stocked my shelves with old books, even though some of them were children's books, and I opened up some of my school books from university so it seemed as if I was studying. I wanted him to think highly of me.

Romy Ronen

I invited Levi over, and of course, he thought I was seducing him, or maybe he just did not want to see me, so I told him my grandfather, a holocaust survivor, was coming over, and he was automatically persuaded. I always needed something to interest him, and surprisingly, it was not my body.

The next day Levi came over an hour before my grandfather arrived. He helped me clean the house and set up for his arrival. It was nice to spend time with him.

When my grandfather arrived, it was somewhat awkward, because he had made the assumption that Levi and I were together. The interaction was odd and misplaced, and Levi wore a sad countenance, which confused me entirely. Once that moment was over, I noticed how well Levi and Halevy got along. It was as if Levi was Halevy's grandson, and I was not a part of it.

As the morning turned to night, however, Halevy spoke truthfully.

"I must confess, I am here for a reason." Halevy said.

"What is it?" Levi asked in anticipation and curiosity.

"I am ill and I do not have much time left."

I dropped the plate in my hand.

When Halevy went to bed, Levi helped me with the dishes. I did not want to cry, but it happened, and I felt ashamed. I had not cried since before Jean died. It felt odd, but Levi comforted me and he was there for me. I went to bed and the air I breathed was suddenly melancholy and sorrowful. Death was not something I handled with grace.

Levi and I took care of Halevy every day. Stacy read him her favorite books. Everything was nice, but it wasn't, because Halevy spent his days knowing that at any moment his life could end. It was so strange to me, watching someone and spending time with them knowing that one day it would no longer be possible. It was miserable and it was momentous in every way possible.

One night, a dark and dreary night, I sang to Halevy when he was in bed. It was a song in Hebrew, because I knew he liked Hebrew better than French or English. The song was 'Eli Eli' written by Hannah Szenes. I sang it to him because my mother and father sang it to me, so I assumed he sang it to my father, or maybe it came from my mother. Either way, I knew he liked the song, so I sang it from my very heart.

"I have to tell you something." He said when the song was finished.

"What is it grandfather?"

"I gave Levi something. Be good to him."

"I do not understand."

"Keep him with you, in your heart. Keep me in there too, along with your parents and your other grandparents. We all live in your heart because it has always been the biggest."

"No, grandfather, Stacy's heart is bigger."

"Non, ma petite fille, yours has always been the biggest. From the day that you were born I saw it in your eyes. Keep everyone in your heart. Even Jean, who I know will always be buried somewhere inside of you. But never Hazel, leave Hazel out of it."

"Je le sais, le grand-père."

"And one last thing. You are smarter and truer than anyone I know. Keep your soul pure."

"I will keep my soul pure." I felt a tear drop on my cheek.

I left the room. I knew that in the morning, my grandfather, Halevy, would be gone forever, in my heart.

"He gave me this ring." Levi said.

A week later, Levi and I were sitting on my couch, looking through photos of my grandparents, including Halevy. Levi reached into his pocket and took out a ring. It was silver and simple; it was my mother's.

"My mother's engagement ring. Why did he give this to you?"

"I have no idea."

I looked at it closely. On the inside of the ring there was an engraving.

"There is an engraving I have never seen before." I said to him.

"What does it say?"

"Je t'aime pour toujours."

"Beautiful."

"Tragic. Those were Jean's last words."

"To you?"

"To me."

Five minutes of misplaced silence passed.

"We have to go to class." Levi said, looking at me with a look I never saw from him before. He put the ring back in his pocket; I did not ask for it.

He opened the wooden door and then closed it behind us. As soon as we were on our way, Joseph and Walter approached me. I had not seen Joseph in weeks, Walter in months.

"What were you thinking, ignoring *me*, your very best friend, for weeks?" Joseph said in rage.

"Who is this?" Walter said, looking at Levi angrily.

"Levi. Je suis heureux de faire votre connaissance." Levi said to Walter, with a cute smile, holding out his hand to shake Walter's.

Walter did not respond nor did he shake Levi's hand.

I ignored the incident and hugged Joseph.

"Je suis desole, Joseph, I was very busy. As for you, Walter, I do not know--"

"What do you not know?" Walter interrupted impolitely.

"We have to go to class. Joseph, I'll talk to you later."
I said.

"Alright, I will call you. Promise me that this time you
will answer." Joseph said.

"I promise." I replied.

It started raining, so Levi opened his yellow umbrella.
The gray clouds cried as Levi and I walked away without
looking back. I could feel Walter's dark gaze behind us, and
it melted me: my hot blood gushed and cascaded into my
soul.

One night, Levi came to my house after class. I went to the kitchen to get a bottle of wine, and when I came back, I found Levi reading my diary. He read an excerpt from something I had written in high school:

Feb. 1960: When I was seven years old I remember feeling old: old and decrepit. The ocean took me by surprise, and it attempted to take me away. It claimed I was poisoned. It claimed I wasn't myself. It claimed I wasn't normal. Every wave dragged me with force, and life wasn't life anymore. I was no longer a little girl. I was a thing, a thing to use and to drag and to abuse. I understood, even at that age, that the ocean was attempting to pull me into oblivion, and I did everything to prevent it from occurring. I remember looking at the ocean's wrinkles and knowing that I had developed them too. I remember looking at the ocean's dark eyes and knowing that I had them too. I remember looking at the ocean's dark soul and knowing that my essence was dark too. And then I realized I was looking at a reflection; the ocean was tricking me into thinking it was my own. I ran away from the ocean and I never looked back. I picked up a mirror and looked at my real reflection. I was the sun; my hair was gold, my eyes were warm, my cheeks were pink. I was never her ocean, nor will I ever be. I was my own.

"Who was that about?" He asked me, without apologizing for violating my privacy.

"Hazel."

"I thought you loved her unconditionally, before-"

"Not always."

"Oh."

"Please stop reading."

"Sorry." He put my journal away.

The next morning I woke up with Levi in my bed, right next to me. I had no recollection of the night before. I got up and left my own house, opened the wooden door, and stepped out into Monte Carlo: rainy and bewildering.

I never asked Levi what had happened because I did not want to assume or presume or speculate or postulate.

The next week, my friends came to visit. They brought champagne and cigarettes, and June's Chanel No. 5 permeated the air. By inviting June, I realized Walter was a given, so I had to deal with his nonsense. But besides him, Levi and Joseph and some other friends filled the night with endless entertainment and pleasure.

By midnight, our minds were so lost that we laughed without shame. I remembered bits and pieces, spasmodic and fitful moments, but the puzzles in my mind were not put together. Around 12:15 am, Levi and I had a conversation that turned everything around. I did not know where we were, but it was outside, by the ocean, maybe, and the sky was filled with effervescent stars and planets. We were lying down on a soft surface, possibly sand, and our heads were stuck together, as our bodies were distant and detached.

"When you look at the stars what do you see?" I asked Levi.

"I see stars." He responded abruptly. I laughed.

"No, I mean, do you see your love or your life or your darkest self? Do you break free or do you face the unknown?"

"None of the above. I see her."

"Who is her?"

"My sister."

"Your sister?"

"Elle est morte."

"What happened?"

"I would not like to discuss it. I was very young. But when I look at the sky, with clouds or with stars, all I see is her and her bright smile."

"What did she look like?"

Levi looked at me, hesitated, but then took out a photo from his wallet. In the picture was a little girl, probably five years old, with light hair and sparkling eyes.

I looked up at the stars. "I see her too." I said.

"No. You see Jean. You will always see Jean."

I looked at the sky again. This time, I saw Levi. But I told him differently.

"You are right. I see Jean." I lied.

The next day I woke up in a hotel room with elegant crystals and empty champagne bottles. Levi, Walter, and Joseph were next to me, asleep, and my mind was racing with attempts to recollect the events from the night before. Then I realized that Stacy was at home, alone, without me. Frantically, I woke everyone up and tried my best to understand where we were. When Walter opened the curtains, opened reality, I thought I was dreaming. Right in front of me was the Tour d'Eiffel. We were in Paris.

I realized that when Levi and I were talking under the sky, possibly the 'ocean,' there was no sky. We were in an airplane.

Then I realized that June was not with us. We called her and she told us everything that had happened, and that Stacy was safe, with her.

This is truly what friends were for. I knew that I could trust my friends to help me remember my mistakes, my risks, and my troubles.

Chapter Four: His Paris

June told us that after we drank a sufficient amount in my house, one of us suggested we go to Paris. She could not remember who, but she assumed Walter, because he was the only one crazy enough to suggest something of that nature. June then decided, responsibly, to stay and take care of Stacy. She said she had no idea how we got a penthouse, in one of the most expensive hotels in Paris, and said that she doubted any of it was legal. When we got off the phone, Joseph asked if he could talk to me alone while Walter and Levi went to get breakfast.

"Gigi, I know who suggested we go to Paris. I remember now."

"Qui?"

"Toi."

"Moi?"

"Toi."

"Why?"

"At one point, you talked to me alone, and you told me that Levi asked to elope with you in Paris."

"Elope?"

"Elope."

"Has he gone mad?"

"He definitely has gone mad."

"So then why did everyone else come?"

"You told him that you did not want to get married without your friends as a way of saying no."

"But did I say no?"

"No."

"Oh, mon dieu."

We spent a whole day together in Paris being carefree. By midnight, I was sitting on a step of a brownstone with Levi.

"I do not want to leave."

He looked at me and laughed. "Nor I."

"L'amour triomphe sur tout à Paris."

"Joseph told you, did he not?"

"How-"

"I knew the moment he asked you to speak alone."

"Oh."

"I was drunk."

"You were very drunk."

"Mais-"

"Mais?"

"I would not have regretted it."

There was a moment of perfect silence.

"We should stay here." I said, breaking through the uncertainty in the air.

"I agree."

"Promissez-vous?"

"Je promis."

He kept his promise. But Walter and Joseph did not. They stayed in Paris too. And to be frank, I was happy they stayed. It was a weight off my shoulders.

We stayed at Abella's, Walter's 'friend,' ex-lover, in Paris. Abella had light blonde hair frazzled in a bun at the top of her head. She wore a red handkerchief to tie her bun, and whenever someone sneezed, she took off the handkerchief and gave it to them. Joseph and I would laugh for minutes every time. Her eyes were small and so were her breasts, which surprised me because Walter barely made love to girls with small breasts, except me.

Her house was grand and splendid, with four bedrooms and a beautiful view of the Tour d'Eiffel. Each room had an intricate specialty, a notable object, and Abella made sure that every room had at least three paintings. Art was her world, her love, and her family.

Joseph and I stayed in one room, and Walter and Levi were in another room. Walter made that decision, and I was fine with it. Besides, I was most comfortable staying with Joseph because he felt like family. He was the only one left, except Stacy.

A couple of nights passed, and Abella took us to her favorite bar in Paris. The night was wild and hysterical. Poets and artists and philosophers filled the crowd with intelligence and freedom. I felt stimulated and high. It was one of the best nights until it was not.

From the corner of my eye, I saw someone who looked hauntingly familiar. A girl with the same blue eyes and the same dark hair. And then I realized who it was. Jean's sister, Jenny. I looked away as soon as I realized who she was, but it was too late. She approached me.

"Gigi!"

"Bonjour, Jenny."

She hugged me. I felt sick to my stomach. Her smell was the same as his.

"How have you been?"

"I am alright, and you?"

"Splendid. Absolutely splendid. I found a beautiful apartment in Paris. Jean would have really loved it. He would have loved it. I have been painting pictures, pictures of Jean. You should come to my apartment and see them. I also have something for you. I forgot to give it to you. You know what? You should come over right now! Please do. Wow, I must be rambling. I ramble when I am drunk. Drunk, drunk, drunk. Ha! Jean loved to get bombed. We used to get bombed together. Did you know that?"

"No. But Jenny, I really cannot come over. I am staying with a mutual friend and I do not know Paris as you do. But maybe another time."

"Stay with me, my love! Just please come."

I really did not want to go. But I knew I had to. I found Joseph and told him I was leaving.

I entered Jenny's limousine. Paris seemed dimmer and quieter from the inside of her limousine's confines. Her house was the most pathetic. It was completely empty, except for paintings of Jean. She was a woman obsessed.

The paintings were dreadful, except for one. It was a painting of Jean's eyes, one pair open and the other pair closed. There were words underneath that said: 'Out of touch, Out of love.' It was the most beautiful art I had ever seen.

"I like this one." I told Jenny, while pointing to the painting.

"Jean painted that one. That was what I was talking about at the bar. It was meant for you as a birthday present but he gave you the necklace instead."

"You should keep it."

"No. Jean would want you to have it."

"Why does it say 'Out of touch, Out of love?'"

"I cannot say."

"Please do. For four years I never understood how he felt. Everything was undefined. I cannot live in this world without knowing his heart."

Jenny sat down. She was carrying the weight of a thousand words. "He hated you for the longest time. I

always thought he was just in love with you, but he kept
insisting that he hated you. He thought you were annoying
and a busy body. I told him not to think that way. I told
him to appreciate you. I told him not to take your love for
granted. So one day he wanted to talk to you about how
much he hated you, but instead he just kissed you. And
then you told him you loved him and he said it back, which
really confused him. He was so confused that he spent the
whole night making that painting as a birthday present. But
I told him not to give it you. I fought with him to give you
something more, something that truly defined how he felt:
the necklace. Are you wearing it?"

"Yes." I took it out from under my shirt. I showed it
to her.

"This must really confuse you."

"None of this matters, Jenny. Jean is dead. Painting
all these pictures of him in an empty apartment will not
bring him back. This does not help anyone. I need to
leave."

"Please, Gigi, do not leave. And please keep the painting."

"Why should I? I am a busy body. I am annoying. He hated me. Why should I stay and keep a painting that represented his hate for me?"

"He obviously loved you. Please, stay."

I looked at Jenny for a long time. I felt I could not breathe. I wanted to cry but I was too angry. I was so frustrated that my skin was burning and my fingers were shaking. My mind was a dizzy delusion and I felt myself being drawn to an alternate reality. But I controlled myself.

"I apologize for the outburst. I will stay."

"Thank you."

We looked at the paintings together all night. We fell asleep on her couch and everything was alright. The next morning I went back to Monte Carlo, breaking my promise to Levi. Jenny came with me.

Chapter Five: My Monte Carlo

Joseph and Walter came back after a couple of days, but Levi never did.

Jenny stayed with me and Stacy for the longest time. Every day felt more sickening. She was a stark reminder of who I was and not who I wanted to be. But her charm swayed me into oblivion, just like his.

I missed Levi every day. The more I saw Jenny, the angrier I was that she deprived me of his company. When a month passed without Levi, I felt I was going to explode. I called Abella, I called hotels I thought he would be staying in, I did everything I possibly could do to find him.

The only thing I did not do was go back to Paris. Paris was Jenny. But Jenny was here. I wanted her to go back more than I wanted to Levi to come back.

Levi was not just a possibility for more, he was my friend first. He was everything Halevy was. He was everything Walter was not. I wanted that back. I wanted family. But I wasted it on Jenny. I wasted it on Jean. I chose Jean, the option that was not an option. I hated myself for doing that.

One night I wanted to hurt myself. I had a dream that Hazel escaped prison. I knew in my heart that the one thing she wanted to do in her pathetic life was kill me. I thought, why not? Why not let the devil kill the angel?

I woke up, and for a moment or two I thought my dream was rational. But then I talked to Jenny. She took care of me like a big sister.

I realized that the world would never let the devil kill the angel. It would never even let the angel kill the devil. Because no matter how evil or good people were, the world was helping them reach their fate.

My fate was not to die young. My fate was my own path, with or without little devils and angels. My fate was Stacy and the university and my friends. My fate was love.

It was a Sunday night. I sat down on the rocks in the ocean, the place I had always imagined as my spot with Jean.

I was wearing a flowy white dress with my mother's pearls. I just wanted to watch the waves, without him.

As I was watching the midnight waves spread their wings, the skies darkened and the moon hid behind the grey clouds.

I heard an echo from the sand below, and I figured it was Joseph or Walter or maybe even Levi. I hoped in all my heart it was Levi, coming back to say hello or to tell me why he had not come back.

I searched for the echo, but I was too high on the rocks to see anything that far low. I was too high for his low.

I decided to gather my things and climb down from the rocks to the surface. My barefoot feet touched the cold sand and I followed the echo. I was close enough to see a figure, but I did not see his face.

I could not believe my eyes. I knew they were lying to me. I knew it was one of my delusional dreams. I knew I was being pulled back.

But was I?

I jumped into my fear and my love and I ran towards the figure. He was wearing a stained white shirt with ripped pants. His eyes were bright but his skin was darker and bloodier. I got closer and closer and I finally reached him.

It was Jean. He hugged me. My heart jumped out of my chest.

"I must be dreaming."

"I have been looking for you, Gigi. I survived."

"What do you mean? This is my mind again. This is my delusion."

"No, Gigi, this is real." He held my hands. I felt his hands. They were real.

His touch made me cry.

"I--"

"After I was shot, everyone thought I was dead. But Hazel abducted me and healed me. She wanted to torture me and cause me severe pain. I managed to run away. But then I came back for you. I was here all along. The memories between us are real. I was there through everything."

That hurt.

"I love you." He said.

Another lie.

"Alright." I said.

"Please--"

"What?"

He kissed me. Time stopped.

"Are you wearing the necklace?" He said.

"Yes." I took it out from under my dress and showed it to him. "I wear it every day."

I was disconnected. I needed a moment to process everything.

"You can come back for good." I said.

"I know."

And then the moment was over. The ultimate question, the life-altering wonder in my mind finally reached a consensus. I was free of myself and my doubts.

"Do you want to?"

"More than anything. But only with you."

"With me?"

"With you."

Made in the USA
Middletown, DE
25 March 2017